BY JAKE MADDOX

Text by
THOMAS KINGSLEY TROUPE

Illustrations by
EDUARDO GARCIA

Jake Maddox books are published by Stone Arch Books
A Capstone Imprint
1710 Roe Crest Drive
North Mankato, Minnesota 56003
www.capstonepub.com

Library of Congress Cataloging-in-Publication Data

Maddox, Jake.
  Gold medal swim / by Jake Maddox ; text by Thomas Kingsley Troupe ; illustrated
by Eduardo Garcia.
      p. cm. -- (Jake Maddox sports story)
  Summary: Sam is the best swimmer on his team, and he is happy to help the new
student, Julien, practice his laps and technique--but when it comes to an actual
race, only one swimmer can win.
  ISBN 978-1-4342-3288-5 (library binding) -- ISBN 978-1-4342-3902-0 (pbk.)
  1. Swimming--Juvenile fiction. 2. Teamwork (Sports)--Juvenile fiction. 3.
Competition (Psychology)--Juvenile fiction. 4. Friendship--Juvenile fiction. [1.
Swimming--Fiction. 2. Teamwork (Sports)--Fiction. 3. Competition (Psychology)--
Fiction. 4. Friendship--Fiction.] I. Troupe, Thomas Kingsley. II. Garcia, Eduardo,
1970 Aug. 31- ill. III. Title. IV. Series.

  PZ7.M25643Gol 2012
  813.6--dc23

                            2011032457

Graphic Designer: Russell Griesmer
Production Specialist: Michelle Biedscheid

Printed in the United States of America in Stevens Point, Wisconsin.
102011
006404WZS12

TABLE of *CONTENTS*

Chapter 1: Like A Fish 5

Chapter 2: The New Guy 13

Chapter 3: Medal Mania 17

Chapter 4: Pro Practice 24

Chapter 5: A Favor 29

Chapter 6: Overheard 34

Chapter 7: The Challenge 40

Chapter 8: Back to the Blocks 46

Chapter 9: A Big Change 53

Chapter 10: A Surprise Win 57

Chapter 11: The Medalist 62

LIKE A FISH

Sam Jacobs dove into the school pool with a small splash, cutting through the water easily. He tried to stay under as long as he could before coming up and beginning his strokes.

When he was underwater, Sam felt relaxed. It was calm and quiet beneath the surface of the pool. Once he came up to breathe, it would be all noise and splashing.

Besides, being underwater meant speed, and speed won races. Coach Berg said that to Sam and the rest of the Rockford Middle School swim team practically every day.

Sam almost made it to the middle of the pool before he came up for air. He surfaced and moved into his crawl stroke. He started off the same every time: *right, left, breathe.* Sam powered across the pool, his arms cutting cleanly through the water.

As he neared the end of the pool, Sam prepared to do a flip-turn. Just before his hand touched the wall, he tucked his chin and pulled his arms to his sides. He went into a somersault and flipped his body over in the water. As he came out of the flip, Sam straightened his arms and brought his hands together. With his knees still bent, he pushed firmly off the wall with his feet.

Sam shot through the water. He could feel the waves from his teammates' kicks in the lanes on either side of him. They were already several strokes behind him.

Sam was the best swimmer on the team, and he knew it bugged some of his teammates. *I'm not going to slow down just because it's practice*, Sam thought.

Sam reached the end of the pool and pulled off his goggles. He hopped out of the water and took a seat on the edge of the pool. Coach Berg walked over, holding his clipboard and stopwatch in one hand. He was grinning.

"Great job, Sam," the coach said. "That's your best time yet." He turned the watch's face so Sam could see his time for the 200-meter freestyle.

"Two minutes and seventeen seconds?" Sam asked. He wiped water out of his eyes.

"Yep," Coach Berg said. "You're going to be pretty hard to beat at the next meet."

The coach walked away to show the rest of the swimmers their times. Drew, one of Sam's teammates, pulled himself up onto the wall in the lane next to Sam.

"Had a bad start," Drew said, wiping water off his face. "I came off the block late. Otherwise, I would've beat you, man."

"A good start makes all the difference," Sam agreed.

He and Drew had been rival athletes for as long as Sam could remember. For a long time, they had traded off getting first and second place. But lately, Sam had been coming in first more often.

Sam knew it bugged Drew to come in second. Drew was extremely competitive. But Sam never liked to rub it in.

Besides, it's not like I'm better at everything, Sam thought. He knew Drew was a better baseball player than Sam could ever hope to be, which was painfully obvious during baseball season.

Still, Sam was proud that his hard work was paying off. *Drew might own the diamond,* Sam thought, *but the pool is mine.*

Coach Berg blew his whistle to get everyone's attention. "Rockford swimmers over here!" he called. "I have an announcement to make."

The Rockford swimmers all stopped talking. They walked over and gathered around their coach.

"Listen up, guys," Coach Berg called, dropping his whistle from his mouth. "We're going to have a new swimmer on the team. He'll be joining us for the final meet of the season."

Sam glanced at his teammates. Everyone looked confused.

"Seriously?" Drew muttered. "Who joins a swim team at the end of the season?"

Sam shrugged. He waited to hear what else the coach had to say.

"I'm sure a few of you have already met Julien Cabrera at school," Coach Berg continued. "But for those of you who haven't, Julien is one of the new exchange students at Rockford this year. He's from Venezuela, and he's excited to have a chance to swim with us."

"Can he even swim?" Drew asked.

"He's a fine swimmer," Coach Berg said. "Besides, he'll only be with us for the last meet."

There was some grumbling from the swimmers standing around the deck of the pool.

Coach Berg blew the whistle. "Okay, okay. That's enough," he warned the team. "Julien will be joining us tomorrow. I want everyone to make him feel welcome. That's all for today."

CHAPTER 2

THE NEW GUY

When Sam hit the locker room the next day, someone was waiting at his locker.

"Are you on the swim team?" the guy asked Sam as he set his bag down.

"Yep," Sam said. "I'm Sam Jacobs." Sam held out his hand.

"Julien Cabrera," the boy said, shaking his hand. "I went into a different locker room first. I think the basketball players were wondering what I was doing there."

"Well," Sam said. "You're in the right spot now. You can always tell when you smell the chlorine." Sam took a deep breath and smiled. "Smells like home."

Julien laughed. Then he and Sam got changed and headed out to the pool.

A few of the other guys gave Julien curious looks as they got closer. Sam tossed his swim cap and goggles on a bench near the pool.

"Do you swim back home?" Sam asked.

"A little bit," Julien admitted. "I've never been on a swim team before. I thought it would be fun and challenge me a bit."

"What sports do you usually play?" Sam asked. He couldn't imagine starting a new sport at the end of the season. Whatever reasons Julien had, it took guts.

"Soccer, track," Julien said. "Sports you don't need a swimming pool for."

Sam nodded. "That's cool," he said. "Well, I hope you like swimming laps, because Coach Berg is all about getting the laps in."

Julien nodded. "I can do a few laps," he said. "No problem."

Sam smiled. *Oh, man*, he thought. *If this guy thinks it's just going to be a few laps, he has no idea what he's in for.*

CHAPTER 3

MEDAL MANIA

All the swimmers headed to their lanes to warm up. When Sam was finished with his laps he stood at the wall catching his breath. A few minutes later, Drew popped up in the lane next to Sam. He smirked at Sam.

"Making friends with the new guy, Sam?" Drew asked. "I still think it's dumb of him to join the swim team right before the final meet."

Sam shook his head. "It's cool," he said. "Julien's a good guy."

"Don't expect me to go easy on him," Drew said. "I don't care how nice he is."

"Nice," Sam muttered. "Really great sportsmanship, man."

Everyone started with a warm-up. They swam a slow-paced 300-meter mix of freestyle, breaststroke, and backstroke.

When the warm-up was finished, Sam moved onto conditioning drills. He started with four 50-meter sets of scissor kicks with both arms extended in front.

Next, the swimmers did four 50-meter sets of arm pulls for each arm. Sam made sure to stay on his side and keep his face down as he used first his right arm, then his left, to pull himself across the pool.

When he came up for air, Sam noticed that Julien was having trouble keeping up. While everyone else swam the drills easily, Julien used a kickboard to keep up.

When practice was over, everyone finished their cool-down laps and headed into the locker room — except Julien. Sam hung back for a moment and watched him swim. As Julien neared the wall, Sam squatted down. He stuck a hand in the water to get Julien's attention.

"Julien," he said. "Practice is over."

Julien reached the wall and pulled his goggles up onto his swim cap. He looked around and saw the rest of the pool was empty. Then he looked back up at Sam.

"I need to finish my laps," Julien insisted. "I have two more."

Sam sighed. "Don't worry about it," he said. "We'll be back tomorrow. Besides, the pool is closing soon."

Julien climbed out and stared at the pool. "I need to get better at this," he said quietly.

"It takes some practice," Sam said. "That's all. Give yourself a break. This was your first day on the team."

Sam headed toward the locker room, hoping Julien would follow. When he didn't, Sam turned and walked back.

"Are you okay?" Sam asked. Julien looked frustrated.

"I will be okay," Julien said. "I just want to do well at the meet."

"I'm sure you'll do fine," Sam said.

"I want to do better than fine, Sam," Julien said. "I want to win a medal."

"That might be tough," Sam said. "Swim meets are pretty competitive."

"You don't think I can do it?" Julien asked.

"I just think you're going to need a lot more practice than what you've had," Sam said carefully. "The last meet is next week."

"I can get better by then," Julien said. "I'll practice as much as I can."

"That's a great attitude," Sam said. "But we only have practice for two hours each night. It's hard to get your speed and technique up in that short a time."

"This is important to me," Julien said. "I've never won anything before. All my brothers back home have, but never me."

"What?" Sam asked. He couldn't believe that Julien had never won anything.

"My soccer team has never made it to the playoffs. I've never gotten better than fourth place in track," Julien admitted. "I always come close, but never close enough."

"Maybe we can do something about that," Sam said. A plan formed in his head. "I can't make any promises, but I've got an idea. Meet me at my house tomorrow after practice."

CHAPTER 4
PRO PRACTICE

"You have a pool?" Julien exclaimed, dropping his gym bag. He stood on the patio in Sam's backyard the next day and stared at the swimming pool.

"Yeah," Sam said. "My dad was a big swimmer back in high school and college. He bought this house because it had a pool."

"You must swim all the time, then," Julien said.

"Not as much during swimming season," Sam admitted. "I get my fill from practice. But I've been in the water since I was around two years old, I guess."

"That must be why you're so fast," Julien said. "You can do laps whenever."

Sam shrugged. He knew just having a pool didn't mean he'd become a good swimmer. He'd put in more time back and forth across the pool than he could count.

"Here's the deal," Sam said. "If you need a place to swim after practice, you're welcome to use my pool."

"Are you serious?" Julien asked, looking to see if Sam was kidding. When Sam nodded, Julien grinned.

"That's wonderful!" Julien said. "Thank you so much."

"I'll help you as much as I can," Sam said with a smile. "But we need to be realistic. It takes a ton of practice and lots of laps to get your speed up."

"I know," Julien said. "But I need to feel like I tried. Can we get started now?"

Sam laughed. "Sure," he said. "Did Coach Berg tell you which event you'll be doing?" Sam asked.

"The 100-meter freestyle," Julien replied.

"Then that's what we'll concentrate on up until the meet," Sam said. "Making sure you swim those four laps as fast as you possibly can."

For the next two hours, Sam helped Julien practice swimming laps. He showed Julien how to be sure to roll his whole body with each stroke.

"Pretend you're a big chunk of meat on a spit," Sam said. "If you don't twist your torso along with your hips, you'll cause drag in the water and slow yourself down."

Julien imitated Sam's movement. It took him a few laps to get the timing right, but when he did, it made a difference.

"I feel faster already!" Julien cried when he reached the wall.

Sam nodded. "It takes a while to master," he said. "When you're nervous and competing in a meet, it's even harder."

"I'll keep trying it, then," Julien said. "Saturday is going to be here in no time."

CHAPTER 5
A FAVOR

A week later, Sam studied the swim meet program in frustration. He'd known Julien was swimming in the 100-meter freestyle. But he hadn't realized he was scheduled to compete against Drew. Sam needed to talk to Coach Berg right away.

Sam found his coach studying his clipboard near the pool. "Sam, what can I help you with?" Coach asked as Sam walked up.

"I just saw the schedule for the meet next week," Sam said. "Julien is swimming against Drew."

"That's right," Coach Berg said. "I wasn't sure where else to put Julien. Drew should do well no matter what, so it won't be a huge loss if Julien doesn't place."

"But Julien's going to feel like he's letting us down if he doesn't do well," Sam said. "There's no way he can beat Drew."

"Sam, we need all the points we can get if we hope to make it to State," the coach said. "I can't change the lineup to help one swimmer. That's not fair to the team. Besides, aren't you working with Julien?"

"Yeah," Sam replied. "We've been practicing at my pool all week. But he's nowhere near ready to race Drew."

"I'm glad you're looking out for your friend, Sam, but this is the lineup," Coach Berg said. "Either Julien swims the 100 or not at all."

Sam didn't have anything to say. He knew Julien would be disappointed if he couldn't swim at the meet.

"Who knows," Coach Berg added. "Maybe Julien will surprise us."

* * *

Back in the locker room, Sam found Drew getting ready to hit the pool.

"Hey, Drew," Sam said. "Hold up for a second. You're doing the 100-meter in Saturday's meet, right?"

"Yeah," Drew said. "So what? It should be an easy win."

"That's the thing," Sam said. "Do you think you could ease up a bit and give Julien a chance? He's working really hard."

"Are you serious?" Drew asked. He shook his head in disbelief. "This is the last swim meet of the season, and you want me to slow down so the new guy can win?"

"I just thought it might be nice," Sam muttered.

"Forget it, man," Drew snapped. He stormed off toward the pool.

That was dumb, Sam thought. *Like Drew would do anything to help a rival swimmer.*

When Sam turned around, he was face to face with Julien. From the look on Julien's face, Sam knew that he'd heard everything.

CHAPTER 6

OVERHEARD

"You don't think I can win," Julien said.

"That's not it," Sam said. "I think you'll do really well. I just wanted to help you."

"Having someone let me win doesn't help me," Julien said quickly. "It doesn't mean anything if I don't win on my own!"

Sam nodded. "I know," he said. "I'm sorry. I just wanted to help you win something. You said you've never won a trophy or anything like that, so . . ."

"I don't want to talk to you right now," Julien snapped. He brushed past Sam and stomped out of the locker room. Sam stood there for a moment and shook his head.

Dumb, he thought. *Really dumb, Sam.*

He quickly changed and headed to the pool. Though he could understand why Julien was so upset, it reminded him of something his dad always said:

No good deed goes unpunished.

Sam had never liked that expression. It sounded like you shouldn't bother doing anything good. Like it was better to do nothing at all. Before then, those words never made sense to him.

Now he wished he'd followed those words and minded his own business.

* * *

During practice, Sam noticed some of the other swimmers glaring at him. He knew Drew had told them about the favor he'd asked. Even Julien found a lane far away from Sam's.

When Sam finished his first set of eight laps, Coach Berg crouched down to show him his time. 2:23:18. He was a full five seconds slower than earlier in the week.

"What's going on, Sam?" Coach Berg asked. He shook his head and reset the timer. "We need you to take the 200 next week."

"I will," Sam promised. "I'm just having a bad day, I guess."

Coach Berg raised his eyebrows and stood up. Without another word, he walked along the edge to time the other swimmers.

This just keeps getting better, Sam thought. He pulled himself out of the pool. He climbed onto the starting block and crouched into position.

He tried to concentrate. *I can do this*, Sam thought. *This is my sport.*

Imagining a starting horn, he dove into the water. He swam underwater as long as he could. When he broke the surface, he took a deep breath and began his strokes.

Right, left, breathe.

In no time, he was at the wall. Sam did a flip turn to reverse direction. His feet planted against the wet tiles and kicked off, shooting like a torpedo through the water.

One down, seven to go, Sam thought. He did all he could to forget everything else and concentrate on his speed.

When he finished, Coach Berg came by with the stopwatch again.

Sam had managed to shave three seconds off of his last time. He groaned. It still wasn't good enough.

With his arms sore and his legs burning, Sam climbed out of the pool. He'd have to try again.

Before he dove back in, he watched Julien finish his four laps. Coach Berg went to show him his time.

It didn't make Sam feel any better to see that Julien looked disappointed, too.

CHAPTER 7

THE CHALLENGE

"Not looking so good, is he?" a voice said behind Sam.

Sam turned around. Drew was standing there, arms crossed.

"Leave Julien alone," Sam said. "You don't want to ease up on him. Fine."

Drew smirked. "I had an idea. We could give him a real taste of what a meet will be like. Why don't we have our own little mini-meet right here?" he suggested.

"Why should we?" Sam asked. "So you can show off before the meet?"

Drew shrugged. "At least this way he'll get used to losing," he said.

Sam shook his head. "I don't think so," he said. "Just get lost."

"Whatever," Drew said. "Figures you'd be too afraid to accept a real challenge."

Sam took a deep breath. He knew Drew was just messing with him. But he couldn't resist. "Fine," he said. "One race, four laps. I'll see if Julien is up to it."

* * *

It didn't take much to convince Julien. "It'll be fun," Sam said, even though he wasn't sure it would be. "You'll get to see what it's like to compete."

"Fine," Julien said. "As long as you guys won't just let me win."

Sam shook his head. "You definitely don't have to worry about that," he said.

Sam, Drew, and Julien took their positions on the starting blocks. When the second hand on the pool clock hit the 12, they were off.

Sam instantly sprang from his block. The other swimmers hit the pool a split second after he did. Sam used his legs to propel him forward, surfacing only when he couldn't stay underwater any longer.

When he broke the surface, Drew was behind him by a few strokes. Sam wanted to beat him even more than usual. He turned on the speed and sliced through the water faster.

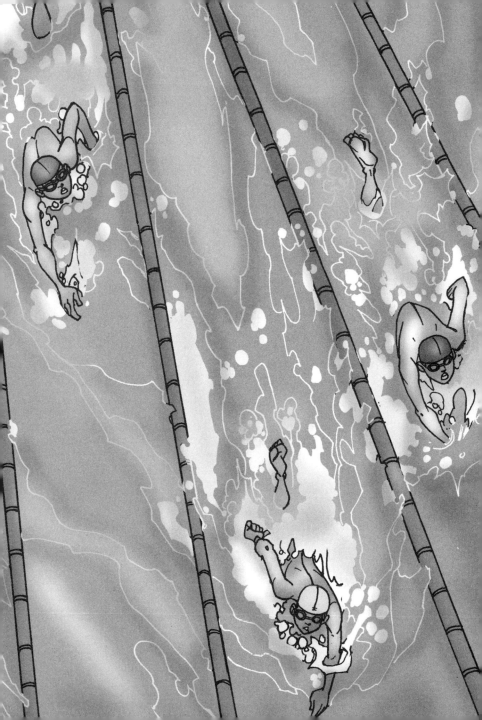

In a few moments Sam was at the wall, turning and heading back toward the blocks. He didn't look to see where Julien was. He could only hope his friend was doing well.

Before long, Sam was tearing down the lane on his last lap. His muscles burned as he swam furiously. He touched the wall and turned. Drew popped out of the water a second later.

He's getting faster, Sam thought.

Looking out at the other lanes, Sam could see that Julien was still half a length behind.

"That's hilarious," Drew said, watching Julien struggle through his last lap. "Seriously. I'm going against this guy at the meet?"

Sam sighed and wiped the water from his face. "He's new," he said. "Besides, he just got done with practice. He wasn't ready for a race."

"And I don't think he'll be ready for the real thing, either," Drew said. "This is going to be like swimming against a kindergartner."

Julien finally touched the wall. He looked around as if to see if there were others still waiting to finish. When he saw Sam and Drew already at the wall, his face sank.

"Maybe this isn't your sport," Drew said to Julien with a nasty smile. "Better luck next time."

CHAPTER 8

BACK TO THE BLOCKS

"Good work," Sam said to Julien as they toweled off.

"That wasn't good," Julien said. "I hesitated and jumped in too late."

Sam shrugged. "I think I can help you with that," he said. "If you still want my help, that is."

"Okay," Julien agreed. "I'm sorry for shouting at you. I know you were just trying to help."

"No, I'm sorry," Sam said. "I shouldn't have doubted you. Don't listen to what Drew says. You're a natural swimmer. Third place isn't bad for your first non-official race."

Julien studied Sam's face, looking for any hint that Sam was joking.

"I'm serious," Sam said. "We just need to work on your start off the block. You'll make up some time there, for sure."

"Tonight?" Julien asked.

"Tonight," Sam said.

* * *

When Julien arrived at Sam's house later that evening, Sam was ready for him. He'd already set up the starting block at one end of the pool. Two small wooden blocks sat near the edge of the water.

"One of the biggest things that improved my time was getting off the block fast," Sam said.

"I know," Julien said. He shook his head in frustration. "That's why I didn't do better in the practice race."

Sam nodded. "That's part of it," he agreed. "The other part is knowing how to angle yourself to hit the water. If you go too deep, it'll slow you down, and then it takes more time to come up for air."

Julien hopped up on the starting block. Sam helped him get into the best position.

"Put one foot up toward the end and hang your toes over the edge. The other foot should be back here," Sam said. He moved Julien's back foot a shoulder's width behind him.

"This is the starting position," Sam said. "You stay here until the starter says, 'On your mark.'"

"I had both feet up close to the edge," Julien said. "That's how some of the guys do it."

"Yeah, but it drives Coach Berg crazy," Sam said. "It's just not a great way to start. You need that kick-off from the back leg to launch yourself."

Sam showed Julien how to crouch down so that his chest touched the tops of his thighs.

"I feel like I'm going to fall forward," Julien said.

"That's the idea," Sam said. He smiled. "I can't tell you how many times I fell in practicing this as a kid."

Sam hit the blocks together to imitate a starter pistol. As soon as Julien heard the sound, he launched himself into the water. Over and over, Sam smacked the blocks, watching as Julien got faster each time.

Once he'd gotten his start down, Sam showed Julien how to do a flip-turn.

"It's all about timing," Sam said. "You have to know when to turn. If you turn too late, your legs get jammed up. If you turn too early, you might not reach the wall."

Julien practiced, shooting for the wall. The first time, he almost forgot to turn at all. He watched Sam do it and tried it again. Together they did it over and over until it became second nature for Julien.

Julien swam lap after lap. Slowly but surely, his time was improving.

* * *

The Friday night before the meet, Sam and Julien raced each other at Sam's pool.

The boys were neck and neck as they swam across the pool. On the final lap, Julien started to draw even with Sam. Sam poured on the speed. He just managed to touch his hand to the wall half a stoke ahead of Julien.

Breathing heavily, Sam pulled himself out of the water and looked over at Julien.

"You're really getting fast," Sam said. He couldn't believe how close the race had been.

"You were going easy on me," Julien protested.

"No," Sam replied, shaking his head. "I wasn't. I really needed the practice."

CHAPTER 9
A BIG CHANGE

"You won't believe this," Julien said when Sam arrived at the swim meet the next morning. "We're both swimming in the same event now."

"What?" Sam said. "Coach Berg is having you swim the 200?"

"No," Julien replied. He pointed to the roster. "He's got us both swimming the 100-meter freestyle."

Sam was stunned. It felt like someone had jerked the floor out from under him. He was about to knock on their coach's door when it opened, and Coach Berg stepped out.

"Before you get upset," Coach said, "this was a last-minute decision. We need at least two swimmers to finish in the top four in the 100-meter. Having you and Drew both in this event helps guarantee that."

Sam slowly let his breath out. He didn't have a problem competing against Drew. But he knew it gave Julien less of a chance to win his event.

"So, I'm up against Drew and you," Sam said to Julien as their coach walked away.

"Is that bad?" Julien asked. He looked confused. "We're on the same team."

"I know," Sam said. "I just thought you'd get a chance to take Drew down on your own."

"It shouldn't matter," Julien said. "Don't hold back, Sam. Promise?"

Sam nodded. "I promise," he said.

Suddenly, having to race Julien didn't seem like a big deal anymore. He knew his friend could hold his own.

No matter what, Sam thought, *our last meet of the season will be interesting.*

CHAPTER 10
A SURPRISE WIN

Sam stepped onto the starting blocks. Julien was a few lanes to his right. When Julien nodded to him, Sam gave Julien a thumbs-up.

Sam turned. Drew hopped up onto the blocks to his left without saying a word. *He's in the zone today*, Sam thought.

"On your mark," the starter called. The swimmers bent over the edge of the pool, holding the edge of their blocks.

Let's get them, Julien, Sam thought. *Right off the block.*

The tone sounded, and Sam shot through the air. He wanted to see how Julien did, but there was no time. Sam dove into the water perfectly, making a tiny splash. His legs kicked as soon as he was in the pool, and he came up fighting.

Right, left, breathe.

Soon he was at the wall. Sam did a flip turn, giving himself a monster push. He surged forward and sliced through the water, pulling himself down the lane. He kicked harder than usual. He knew that since he was only swimming 100 meters, rather than the 200 meters he'd trained for, he'd need to be faster right away. He didn't have to pace himself so he'd have something left on the final lap.

He wondered for a moment how Julien was doing, but he knew he had to focus.

Sam's arms and legs burned as he headed into his last lap. He could hear the crowd going crazy. People were cheering and whistling. Considering the meet was at home, filled with Rockford fans, it had to mean he was in the lead.

Sam pushed himself as hard as he could. Within seconds, he felt his hand touch the wall. *Finally*, Sam thought. The race was over!

Sam tore his goggles off and looked over at Drew's lane. His rival smacked his hand against the water and shook his head. Sam didn't know if Drew had been expecting an easy win, but he could see that Drew wasn't happy.

Sam glanced up at the scoreboard that showed each swimmer's time by lane number.

Wait a second, Sam thought. He squinted at the board. For his lane, it posted his time of 1:05.05. There was a number two next to it. Second place.

"I came in second?" Sam asked out loud. Something wasn't right. He knew he'd beaten Drew. When he checked Drew's time, he was right. Drew had placed third. Sam suddenly understood why Drew was so angry.

Then who got first? Sam wondered. He was trying to find the number one on the scoreboard when he heard Julien shout.

CHAPTER 11

THE MEDALIST

It took Sam a moment to realize what had happened. Julien had beaten them both!

Sam grinned and pulled himself out of the water. He hurried over to edge of the pool. Julien was still in the water, his arms up over his head.

"Congratulations, man!" Sam shouted.

Sam reached down and grabbed his friend's hand, pulling him out of the pool.

The rest of the team crowded around, slapping Julien on the back and high-fiving him.

Even Drew gave Julien a small smile and nod. "Good job, new kid," he said. "I didn't think you had it in you."

Coach Berg had a huge smile on his face. "We're going to State!" he shouted.

* * *

Once the meet was over, Sam showered and changed in the locker room. He was tired and sore, but felt incredible. Julien had won his first event! Better yet? They were going to State!

Sam opened the door to the hallway. Julien was standing outside, waiting.

"I can't believe it, Sam," Julien said. "I got my medal."

Sam looked at the gold medal hanging around Julien's neck and smiled.

"You deserve it," Sam said. "I've never seen anyone work as hard as you to chase one of those down."

"I couldn't have done it without you," Julien said. He grinned. "I can finally say I've won something."

"And you can say you beat some of the fastest swimmers in the district," Sam added. "That's a really big deal."

"So, state championships," Julien said. "Sounds like fun."

Sam nodded. "It's going to take a lot of work, though," he said. "This is the big time. And it looks like I need to up my game."

Julien smiled. "So let's practice," he said.

ABOUT THE AUTHOR

Thomas Kingsley Troupe writes, makes movies, and works as a firefighter/EMT. He's written many books for kids, including *Legend of the Vampire* and *Mountain Bike Hero*, and has two boys of his own. He likes zombies, bacon, orange Popsicles, and reading stories to his kids. Thomas currently lives in Woodbury, Minnesota, with his super-cool family.

ABOUT THE ILLUSTRATOR

Eduardo Garcia has illustrated for magazines around the world, including ones in Italy, France, United States, and Mexico. Eduardo loves working for publishers like Marvel Comics, Stone Arch Books, Idea + Design Works, and BOOM! Studios. Eduardo has illustrated many great characters like Speed Racer, the Spiderman family, Kade, and others. Eduardo is married to his beloved wife, Nancy M. Parrazales. They have one son, the amazing Sebastian Inaki, and an astonishing dog named Tomas.

GLOSSARY

competitive (kuhm-PET-uh-tiv)—very eager to win

concentrate (KON-suhn-trate)—to focus your thoughts and attention on something

medal (MED-uhl)—an award given to someone as a prize for a sporting achievement

obvious (OB-vee-uhss)—easy to see or understand

rival (RYE-vuhl)—someone against whom you are competing

technique (tek-NEEK)—a method or way of doing something that requires skill

torpedo (tor-PEE-doh)—an underwater missle that explodes when it hits a target

trophy (TROH-fee)—a prize or an award such as a silver cup or plaque given to a winning athlete or team

DISCUSSION QUESTIONS

1. Do you think Sam made the right decision when he tried to get Coach Brady and Drew to go easy on Julien? Talk about your opinion.

2. Julien is an exchange student visiting from Venezuela. If you were an exchange student, what country would you want to visit? Why?

3. Talk about what it means to say, "No good deed goes unpunished." Do you think that saying is right? Why or why not?

WRITING PROMPTS

1. Julien was really upset when he overheard Sam talking to Drew in the locker room. Imagine you're Julien, and rewrite the scene from his point of view.

2. Julien joins the swim team, even though he's not a great swimmer. Write about a time you tried something new.

3. Sam thought he was helping Julien out by asking Drew to let him win, but Julien was really angry. Write about a time you thought you were doing the right thing, but it backfired.

MORE ABOUT
SWIMMING

Swimming has been an official sport at every modern Summer Olympic Games. Although the sport has changed since the Olympics first began — swimming competitions for the first four Olympic Games were held in open water rather than a pool — swimming is still one of the most popular Olympic events. Here are a few of the swimmers who make it famous:

▶ MARK SPITZ

Mark Spitz is a retired American swimmer who once held the record for most gold medals won in a single Olympics. Spitz won seven gold medals at the 1972 Munich Olympic Games, setting new world records in each event. He was the most successful athlete at the Games. In addition to his seven gold medals in Munich, Spitz also won two team gold medals in the 1968 Mexico City Olympics, as well as individual silver and bronze medals.

▶ IAN THORPE

Australian swimmer Ian Thorpe became the youngest swimmer to ever represent Australia in 1997, when he was only 14 years old. When Thorpe began training at eight years old, he was allergic to chlorine, but luckily outgrew his allergy. During his career, Thorpe won five Olympic gold medals, the most won by any Australian swimmer. He also has two silver medals and won the most medals out of any athlete at the 2000 Summer Olympics in Sydney, Australia.

▶ MICHAEL PHELPS

At the 2008 Summer Olympics in Beijing, China, American swimmer Michael Phelps won a record eight gold medals in a single Olympic Games, breaking the previous record held by Mark Spitz. Phelps has been named World Swimmer of the Year six times and American Swimmer of the Year eight times. In total, Phelps has won 14 gold medals. He is the only swimmer to have done so.

THE **FUN** DOESN'T STOP HERE!